Copyright © 1998 by Nord-Süd Verlag AG, Gossau Zürich, Switzerland
First published in Switzerland under the title *Die Nicolais*.
English translation copyright © 1998 by North-South Books Inc.

First published in the United States, Great Britain, Canada,
Australia, and New Zealand in 1998 by North-South Books,
an imprint of Nord-Süd Verlag AG, Gossau Zürich, Switzerland.

Distributed in the United States by North-South Books Inc., New York.

Library of Congress Cataloging-in-Publication Data is available.
A CIP catalogue record for this book is available from The British Library.
ISBN 1-55858-961-9 (TRADE BINDING)
1 3 5 7 9 TB 10 8 6 4 2
ISBN 1-55858-962-7 (LIBRARY BINDING)
1 3 5 7 9 LB 10 8 6 4 2
Printed in Belgium

For more information about our books, and the authors and artists
who create them, visit our web site: http://www.northsouth.com

The
Special
Gifts

BY Peter Grosz

ILLUSTRATED BY
Giuliano Lunelli

TRANSLATED BY
Rosemary Lanning

North-South Books

NEW YORK · LONDON

ONCE UPON A TIME there was a king who enjoyed great
wealth but made his people very poor. He had even ordered
his servants to catch all the wild animals in his kingdom, except for
the wolves. By day the wolves rampaged through the forest, and at
night their eyes glowed eerily through the dark pines.

At the edge of the forest stood a small cottage where an old woman lived. Her back was bent from years of toil, and her hair had turned white. She was very poor, but she had a son whom she loved very much.

Her son sat at home all day, stitching poems onto long sheets of cloth. Now and then, someone came and bought a poem or two, but the money they paid was never enough to feed two hungry mouths.

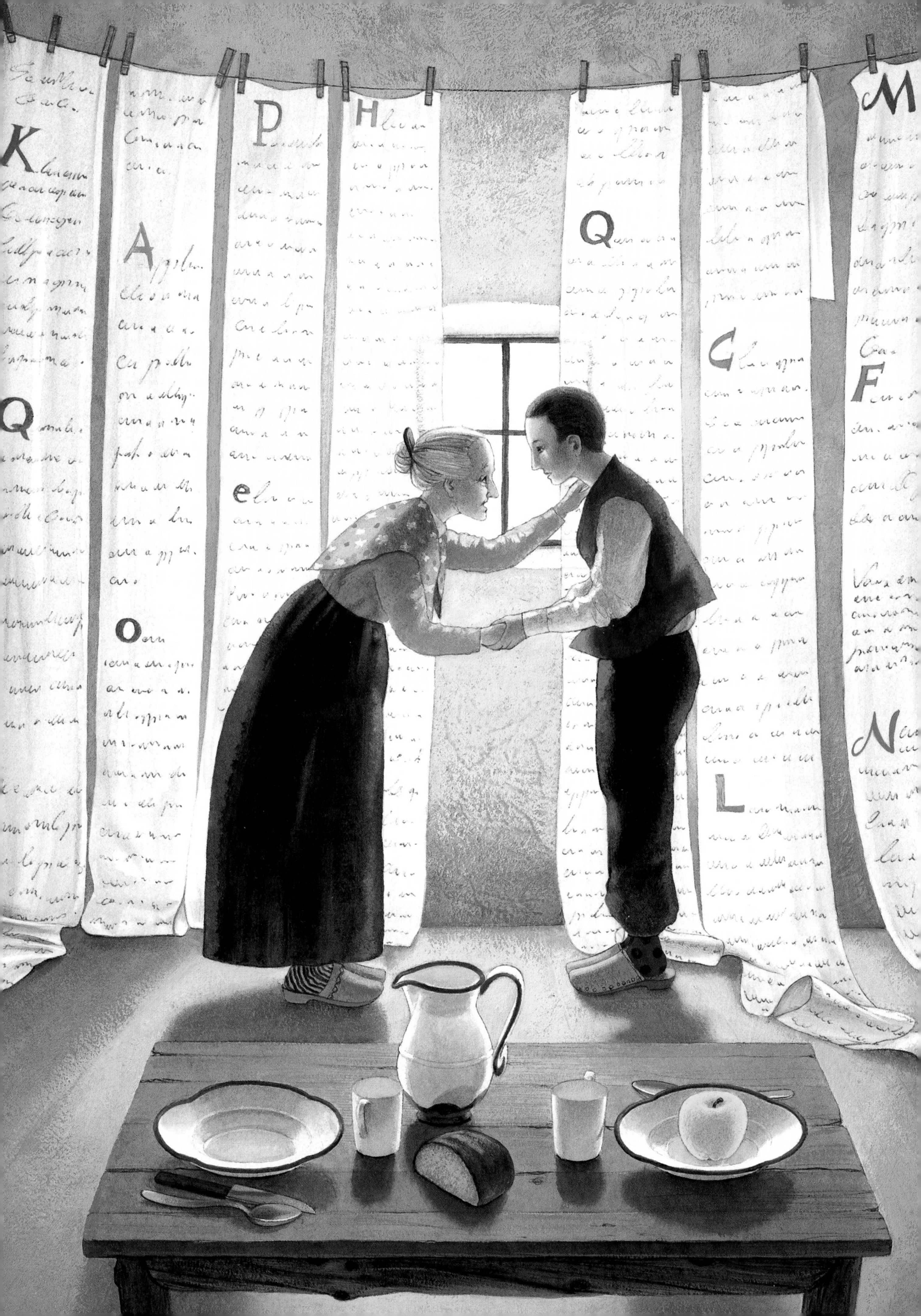

As winter approached, the nights grew colder, and the wolves howled louder than ever. The old woman looked at her empty cupboards and came to a painful decision.

She called her son and said to him, "Nicholas, my dear, you stitch poems beautifully, but you cannot stay here forever. You must find a place of your own. Take what is yours and go out in the world. Find a place where people value fine poetry, where bread is plentiful, and ice does not darken the window. My prayers will go with you."

Nicholas did as his mother bid him and went on his way. The old woman stood at her door, waving, until he was out of sight.

Nicholas ignored the snarling wolves as he walked
away from the forest, over the snowy fields and on,
towards wooded hills.

Soon he came to a larger forest, and as he approached it he heard tearing and rasping noises.

"Is anyone there?" called Nicholas anxiously.

A man stepped out from behind a tree and said, "Yes, it's me, Nicolo the carpenter. Greetings, my friend."

Nicholas was glad to have company in this strange land. He invited Nicolo to travel with him, and Nicolo readily agreed.

It was not long before they met another man. He was sitting under a tree, rubbing stones together.

"Good morning, my friends. Nikolai the stonemason, at your service!" said the man.

Nicholas was delighted by the stonemason's hearty greeting and invited Nikolai to join them too.

So began the friendship of the three Nicks, a friendship that grew stronger and stronger year after year.

The three men built themselves a house deep in the forest, each contributing his special gift. Nicolo the carpenter bent and shaped wood. Nikolai the stonemason cut and trimmed stones, and Nicholas stitched sheets of poems for their new home.

When their house was built and furnished, they shared the household chores. Nikolai the stonemason became the cook. Nicholas the poem-stitcher went out hunting. And Nicolo the carpenter tidied the house and tended the small garden. Every night at supper they told each other stories.

The years passed quickly and the three friends grew old together contentedly.

By the time Nicholas, Nicolo, and Nikolai were very, very old, their hair and their beards had grown long and white, and they looked so much alike that you would think they were brothers. Over the years, living together under the same roof, working together, eating together, telling each other stories, they had grown closer and closer. They thought alike, spoke alike, and hardly needed to tell one another what they were thinking.

One night, as the three old men sat by their crackling fire, Nicholas suddenly sighed. "Oh, dear me," he said.

"Oh, dear me," echoed Nicolo and Nikolai.

And they all shook their heads.

"We seem to have gone wrong somewhere," said Nicholas. "Our lives are easy, yet something is missing."

"I am a carpenter, but I do no woodworking," said Nicolo.

"I am a stonemason, but I do no stonework," said Nikolai

"Words are my craft, but I do not stitch a single poem," said Nicholas.

"Oh, dear me," murmured all three. "We have ignored our special gifts."

"And yet I could still make things from wood," said the carpenter.

"And I things of stone," said the stonemason.

"And I could stitch new poems together," said Nicholas.

"Yes indeed," said the other two.

And they decided that's just what they would do.

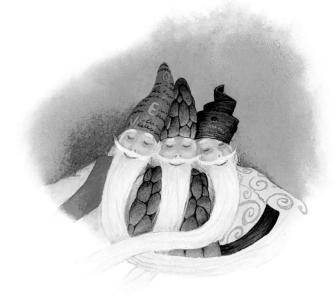

For many days after that Nicholas stayed indoors, Nicolo went into the forest, and Nikolai went down to the river.

At night as they sat by the crackling fire, Nicholas stitched words, bound them together, and sewed covers on them to make book after book.

Nicolo took pieces of wood, then shaped them into boats, planes, and locomotives, each finer than the last.

Nikolai sat, surrounded by stones, and carved them into lifelike animals, fish, and birds.

The old men did not talk. They just smiled.

One morning all three said, "This is better!" And a little while later they said, "But it could be better still."

"Let us share our gifts," said Nicholas. "Like our namesake, St. Nicholas himself!"

"Yes, indeed!" replied Nicolo and Nikolai.

Then, without another word, each of them filled a large sack. They heaved the sacks onto their shoulders, closed their door behind them, and trudged through the snow, from house to house, leaving gifts at every one.

Children heard them coming and stood at their windows, eagerly calling, "Here they come! Here come the three old Nicks!"

And so it continued, year after year,
and as far as I know, the three old Nicks
still go happily about their work, still sharing
their special gifts, and I hope they always will.